BROKEN

BROKEN

ASHLEY POOLE

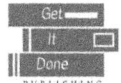

PUBLISHING

Broken

by Ashley Poole. Copyright © 2020

Trade Paperback ISBN: 978-1-952561-01-6

Edited by Get It Done Publishing, LLC.
Atlanta, GA 30349
Ashley King, Publisher

Printed in the USA
Join our Get It Done Readers Group for
sneak previews, updates, new projects, and giveaways.
Sign up at www.getitdonepublishing.com

CONTENTS

Chapter One

BLESSED AND PAID

"No, stop, please stop!" Meagan swung left and swung right. "Get off of me NOW!" she yelled.

"You don't have to do this!" Meagan begged. As she fought, the man pulled her skirt up to insert his penis, and at that moment, she jumped up out of her sleep—another nightmare. Her eyes bulged out as she sat up with her clothes drenched in sweat. She breathed deep, heavy, breaths, and started to cry. She screamed out loud, "Meagan, get up, not today! You will not take pity in your sorrows."

Meagan got dressed and hopped into her 2020 Mercedes Benz G-Class. It was a hot summer day in Atlanta, and although she was running late for work, she decided to stop by her favorite breakfast spot, Flying Biscuit. When she walked through the door, the cashier yelled, "Hey, Meagan, girl."

"Good morning James, I'm going to order my usual to go please," she replied.

"I have a garden-fresh veggie scramble, with a side of

creamy, dreamy grits, and a hot tea coming right up," James responded.

After about ten minutes, James called her up to grab her food. She dropped a twenty-dollar bill in the tip jar and winked, "Thanks James, you're the best."

Meagan passed Brian's parking spot as she pulled in the parking garage of her job. His name was displayed in large font as if he was the damn CEO of the company. Meagan rolled her eyes, "Motherfucker," she spat. She claimed one day she would have a parking spot reserved for her as the vice president of the company. It wasn't a big deal, but it was the principal. Over the years, she had created and hosted training classes for employees and was both capable of filling the position and qualified for the job. She had every intention to be successful and refused to let the white men in the office continue to take over in top positions, just for her to be used to train them.

She parked about eight cars down from Brian's spot, which got underneath her skin even more, but she resolved to be the bigger person and work hard to get what was rightfully hers. She got out of the car and adjusted her outfit as she proceeded to the front door.

She greeted Tony, the security guard who always smiled at her when she walked through the swinging door of the office building. As Meagan waited for the elevator, Tony admired her from afar. He liked the way she walked in heels and the way she exuded confidence.

The doors opened to her floor, and there was Meagan's assistant Alexis, heralding her with a whisper that the president of the company was in her office. Meagan worked for Genesis Investments for years and rarely saw the president in person; this had to be serious, she thought. Alexis explained how she tried calling her several times, but her phone kept going to voicemail. Meagan gathered her thoughts, fixed her clothes, flipped her hair, and proceeding quickly into her office.

"My apologies Mr. Grant for my tardiness, I wasn't expecting you today," she added.

Mr. Grant glanced at his watch and quickly got to the point. Meagan sat at her desk with her legs crossed. She wasn't sure what to expect, but she refused to let him see her sweat.

"It's not a good look for the senior vice president to arrive late to work, what type of example is that?" he asked.

"You can be assured that it won't happen again...pardon me?" she leaned forward with a confused expression, "Did I just hear you call me the senior vice president?"

"Yes, indeed, Meagan. You have done an excellent job over the years and saved our asses on several occasions. I can't imagine anyone else filling the position," Mr. Grant replied.

She kept her composure, walked over to him, and shook his hand. "This is major and what I have been working so hard for! Thank you," she expressed with excitement.

"Congratulations, Meagan Parks. I look forward to your boldness and bright ideas in upcoming meetings. I have high expectations, and I am convinced you will take Genesis to the next level. Don't disappoint me," he added.

"Of course not," Meagan replied with a huge smile.

She watched him as he walked down the hall and into the elevator. She shut the door and took off her leopard red bottoms and yelled, "Alexa, play Lizzo, *Good As Hell*."

Alexis walked into Meagan's office and asked, "What was the unexpected visit about? Is someone getting a promotion or fired?"

3

"Yes, both," Meagan responded, nodding her head. "I got promoted as the senior vice president!" she yelled.

They grabbed each other's hands and jumped up and down a few times before stopping to catch their breaths. Meagan was a hard-working woman with high expectations. She worked hard and played equally as hard; that is what Alexis loved about her boss. She was a woman of power that wasn't afraid to let her hair down. Meagan asked Alexis to pass the Tequila from the Whiskey bar that was displayed in the corner of her office. When Meagan had meetings with big-time investors, she made sure to offer them the finest whiskey. Being a natural-born charmer, she made sure she had options to cater to their liking. It was a bit early for a drink, but the moment called for a shot.

Meagan poured their drinks, and they toasted. Without hesitation, Meagan took her shot to the head and then asked Alexis to call her girls because it was going to be a night of celebrating. Alexis got up and took her shot to the head as well. As she was leaving out the door, she looked at Meagan and said, "I am so damn proud of you. You deserve this promotion more than anybody in this office. Brian is going to be pissed!" They both burst out laughing.

Meagan gathered her things and headed for the door, the heck with work today. She didn't have any important meetings lined up and felt the new senior vice president earned an early day; plus, she had to stop by Lenox for an outfit for her night out on the town. She asked Alexis to jot down all her calls and gave her permission to leave for the day at noon. Meagan walked out of the office as if she had won a million bucks.

She put her shades on, punched the gas, and sped off. She was ready for whatever was coming her way. She knew once Alexis got ahold of her girls, they were going to be calling her immediately. Her phone rang and on three-way were her three best friends: Destiny, Keisha, and Liz. Meagan burst out laughing because all she could hear in unison was, Congratulations, Sis!

"Thanks, gals," she replied. "I want ya'll to be ready at eight tonight. Paul will be coming by to pick ya'll up at Destiny's house. I can't wait!" she exclaimed, fired up with excitement.

Chapter Two

FOREVER SISTERS

*D*estiny was thick and curvy, brown-skinned, with long gorgeous hair. She was always about her coins and loved fashion. She was offered a position in New York and was preparing for her move to the big city. Young, smart, and single, it was nothing for her to pack up and go wherever she wanted.

Keisha was dark-skinned, with naturally long curly hair, curvy, with a big butt that just seemed to get her in trouble. Keisha had four children, and they all had different daddies. Chance, her third child's father, was the only one who stepped up and did his part. At times, he would even help with the other three children since their daddies were missing in action or locked up in prison. Keisha was the one that had the most trying time figuring out life, but you would never know it since she had such an optimistic outlook. No matter what she was dealing with, she made sure her babies were taken care of.

Liz was a light-skinned, short, slim girl with chinky eyes, and had a little girl named Brooklyn. Brooklyn's father was one of them peek-a-boo negros, come when it was convenient for him, but nowhere in sight when Liz needed him. She had just purchased her first house in Marietta and was dating a sweet guy named Derrick who had come into her life and changed all her tears to golden smiles. She was happy, and Meagan was happy for her.

They had all been friends since seventh grade. Destiny and Meagan had lived in the same apartment building while Keisha and Liz lived in the same neighborhood, different buildings, but all off Hambrick Road. They got a kick out of screaming "Brick Road!" as if they owned it. The young dudes in the neighborhood were just as proud, but nobody owned shit. Nevertheless, they represented the east-side heavily.

Keisha and Meagan didn't get along at first because Keisha was very loud, ghetto, tomboyish, and acted just like a dude when they were at the bus stop in the mornings. One day, Keisha's mom asked Meagan's mom if Keisha could stay overnight because she had to take care of something important and wanted to make sure Keisha got off to school on time the following day. Word on the street was Miss Jazzy was tricking and on drugs, so every week, Keisha was always at somebody else's house. Meagan was upset about the request because they didn't like each other and were complete opposites. Meagan was quiet and to herself, while Keisha was loud and louder. Keisha was always cussing people out and fighting about something or laughing extremely loud about everything. Her laugh was deep and annoying. *If only she would just shut up at times,* Meagan would think. That night she came over, they were both not feeling the idea, but were reverent.

Once they started to talk, they got to know each other a little better. After talking for hours, Keisha felt comfortable enough to tell Meagan about a recent incident that took place when she slept over at another friend's house. Keisha vented how her friend's father, who was a cop, raped her. He took her virginity and threatened to kill her if she told anyone. She hadn't shared that with anyone but needed to say it out loud and needed to be comforted. Keisha felt Meagan's serene spirit, and it made her feel a little better by telling her. Keisha had finally found someone she thought she could trust and talk to. Her story encouraged Meagan to share her experience. Meagan didn't want her to feel embarrassed or alone, so she told her about a similar experience she had when a relative came to live with her family took her innocence.

Meagan was a night owl, and so was Mike, who was seventeen at the time. They would sit up talking, watching television, and pulling pranks on each other. One night, however, a playful moment turned to soft touches and kind words. Mike playfully pushed Meagan on the couch. She landed on her back but with her feet still placed on the floor. Mike got on top of her and whispered *it would be okay* as he rubbed her leg and began to pull her pants down. Meagan laid back surprised, confused, and scared.

When he put his penis inside of her, her body got tight, and she gripped the couch from the pain. He proceeded until he was completely inside of her, breaking her hymen, stripping her from her innocence. He moved slowly until he climaxed. Meagan had just turned thirteen and got her menstrual that summer; I guess he smelt the stench of womanhood. She was still just a little girl and had no idea what to do or how to communicate what was going on, so she said nothing.

Night after night, Mike would playfully work his way to a position where he could get in his night of pleasure. Meagan began to pick up his pattern and would try to get in the bed early even when she wasn't sleepy, but he would pull her into the living room, refusing no as an answer. One night, Meagan's dad fell asleep in the living room, so Mike had to find another location in the apartment. Mike guided her to the hallway near her brother's room but positioned her at an angle her dad couldn't see just in case he woke up. Meagan's brother's bedroom door was ajar, so she was nervous.

This night he wanted her to ride him, so Meagan got on top as he held her waist to move her body up and down. As he moved her slowly, the moonlight from the bedroom window lit up a silhouette of a head that popped up. She laid down quickly on the side of Mike's body on the floor until her brother put his head back down. As her heart raced, she crawled quickly into her room, afraid of what may happen next.

The next day Meagan went about her day as usual. Meagan was outside playing with her friends when her mom called her to come inside. As she entered the living room, there they were, her mom, dad, and Mike sitting down on the couch. Mike's demeanor screamed that something was wrong. Meagan already knew.

Meagan's mom addressed her and began to ask questions. Meagan was full of embarrassment. It was as if she was having an out-of-body experience as she watched herself cry, and regretfully answered her mother's questions. Meagan blamed herself, so she spared the details on how she felt about the situation. She spent many nights crying and hoping what was going on would be revealed, but it just never seemed to happen. Now that everything was out. Meagan believed it was over.

However, Mike wasn't kicked out. Her parents just asked Meagan to let them know if he tried something again.

Meagan nodded, but her heart hardened partially with anger and resentment. This is not what she expected, nor wanted. Meagan didn't want to have to face him and live with guilt and shame. She wanted it to be done with.

But when Mike tried it again, Meagan didn't say anything. She felt like her parents didn't care because they allowed him to stay the first time. But shortly after Mike started back, Meagan was asked again if he had tried anything with her, and she confessed he had. Her parents finally kicked him out after realizing he wasn't going to stop. At thirteen, she had become a young woman and had to learn how to move in silence and swallow her pain. It was the beginning of a difficult journey of understanding herself and life.

When Meagan finished telling Keisha her story and all the explicit details, they were both crying, and their noses were full of snot. This was a moment where they first shared their darkest truths and trusted each other to hold their secrets. They promised each other not to tell anyone. That night of restored healing is what bonded them to a lifetime of friendship.

*M*eagan's driver, Paul, called up to the condo to let her know he had arrived, and her girlfriends were also there waiting anxiously. As the driver opened the door, they all started screaming with excitement. Life had taken over, and they were all so busy they never have the chance to meet up as often as they desired; however, they talked every couple of weeks or so. But tonight, they planned to party like it was 2006 on a Sunday night at Mama's Primetime. They pulled up at Tongue and Groove, a sophisticated nightspot in Buckhead. Paul stepped out of the driver's seat to let them out, and the bouncer at the door escorted them to the VIP section for the night, after confirming Meagan's reservation. As they walked through the club, they captured several looks.

Destiny was wearing a gold bandage sequin dress with gold, red bottoms. Her natural hair was bone straight, touching the top of her curvy ass. Keisha had on a pair of black tights with two-inch ankle boots because her ass couldn't last a minute in heels, a see-through leopard top with a black bra exposing her double D bust. Keisha sported her naturally curly hair that brought out her smile and natural beauty. Liz wore a black spaghetti-strap dress with open-toe shoes, and her hair pulled up in a bun with her goldish highlights bringing out her skin complexion. Meagan rocked a burgundy lace spaghetti strap see-through top with a short burgundy skirt that had a split that stopped at her pelvic area. Meagan loved her a mean bob, and you better believe her hairstylist Asia styled her hair for the gawds! She wore her nude Kate Louis Vuittons, her favorite pair of pumps. The females were hating, and the men were choosing.

Tequila shots back to back. They were cracking jokes and talking mess about some of the girls that walked by like they were all of that and a bag of chips, but they looked like muckmaggats. It was like they never skipped a beat when they were around each other. After four shots of Tequila and smoking hookah, Meagan felt someone looking at her. She couldn't see who it was at first, but he started to walk toward their direction. She whispered to Liz and asked, "Do you see that tall, slim, light-skinned guy walking over here with shades?"

"Yeah, he looks familiar," Liz said.

As he got closer, Keisha's loud ass yells, "Look at Charles sexy ass! He still looks good and could always dress."

He approached with a big bright smile. "Hey Meagan, how are you doing?" he asked. Meagan stepped down to the floor and hugged him. As he checked her out, he gave her a twirl, it was obvious she was doing very well for herself. He complimented her and suggested they meet up one day for lunch. Before completing his sentence, Meagan quickly declined, expressing how busy she was.

Charles was Meagan's high school sweetheart, the love

of her life, her everything, so she thought. He was that guy that made her feel special as quiet and shy as she was back in high school. Charles would surprise her with all types of gifts. The older girls would side-eye her for it because he could have been dating one them, but there he was dating a sophomore. Charles was a senior and loved doing things to make her feel and look good. On Valentine's Day, when he showed up to school, he had huge balloons and a life-size teddy bear. Everybody was talking about it, and the girls made slick comments during Spanish class. Meagan was on cloud nine and blurred out all the hate that day. Charles was a guy of surprises, and she loved that about him.

After she graduated from high school, Meagan moved out of her parent's house because she wasn't getting along with her mom, that's when she and Charles got their first apartment together. Three years of being together, yet all it took was six months to tear them apart after moving in with one another. They had no idea about adulthood or what it was like to manage and pay bills, let alone hold down decent jobs. They were young with no guidance. When they started to have financial issues, all hell broke loose. Charles would leave her at home every Sunday to go skating or to the nightclubs with his boys.

He was more outgoing, while Meagan was a homebody and not old enough to get into a lot of the places he went. Those nights out with the boys and more frequent arguments led him into the arms of another woman. That woman became the mother of his first child; the way he broke the news to her was so disturbing. It was around the time when Usher came out with his hit record, *Confessions*. One night, Charles was tipsy and blurted out he got another woman pregnant during an argument he and Meagan were having and ended it with, "that's some confessions for your ass."

Meagan sat on the edge of the bed in disbelief. She even had him call the woman. As Meagan sat on the phone with her asking questions, the female voice was strong, confident, and had no remorse. It left Meagan heartbroken, in pain, lonely, and feeling like she had been stabbed in the back for the first time in her life. She refused to go back home and didn't know what she was going to do. She convinced herself they could get through it together until she caught a bitch in their apartment.

Meagan got a call from her neighbor, who had a crush on her, stating a girl had come to the house accompanying Charles. At first, he thought it was Meagan, but when he realized it wasn't, he called her to see if she knew that Charles was bringing a female home late in the night. Meagan had left home earlier that evening to stay with a girlfriend because she and Charles had gotten into a huge argument. Meagan couldn't believe what she was hearing. She told her girlfriend Toya what her neighbor told her, and they pulled up at the apartment, but Meagan couldn't get in. She kept banging on the door and window until she almost kicked the door down. Charles finally came opening the door, acting like he was sleep. Meagan pushed passed him, searching high and low until she reached the laundry room, and there she was, standing on top of the dryer.

Meagan grabbed her shirt and slung her into the washing machine. She drug her through the kitchen and into the living room, punching her viciously until Charles grabbed her arms, trying to hold her back. Her adrenaline was rushing, she turned around and pushed him onto their glass table, breaking it. He quickly got up running behind her as she reached for a butcher knife. He grabbed her arm, holding her tight until she calmed down. She finally dropped the knife and fell to her knees and began to cry hysterically. Her friend Toya rubbed her back, pulled her up, and led Meagan to her car. Meagan was done, although she didn't want to be, she had to be for her sanity.

Seeing him in the club just gave her chills. It was good to see he was doing well, but she wasn't interested in his request for lunch at that moment. However, she was feeling herself and joined him on the dance floor. Anyone who knows Meagan knows she won't turn down a moment to dance. As they danced three songs straight, he asked if he could buy her a drink. They walked over to the bar, and she asked for vodka and cranberry juice along with a shot of tequila. It was a celebration, so she was soaking it all in. As he attempted to have a conversation, she became very annoyed because she couldn't hear a word he was saying over the music. He guided her by placing his hand on her lower back to direct her to a quieter spot. They laughed, shared stories, life challenges, and successes. He looked at her as he fired up his blunt, and instantly, she became little Meagan that remembered why she was so crazy about him. He puffed his joint and asked if she wanted to join him at the next spot? With a little hesitation, she accepted. As they walked over to her section, she told her girls she was heading out with Charles, and Paul, her driver, would take them home when they were ready. They hugged, and Keisha yelled out, "Fuck it up, Sis!"

Meagan was so embarrassed, but they all knew what time it was. Charles and Meagan pulled up to a small lounge setting where they played pool, smoked hookah, and had a couple more drinks. After getting her ass whooped, he walked over to her and kissed her on the forehead and asked if she was ready to go. They left and went to his loft. It was such a bachelor's pad, but it was nice and clean with black and white decor. He had a black chalk wall that was full of comments from his friends; Meagan wrote, "Love is Life."

He smiled, walked over and picked her up with each hand gripping an ass cheek. She wrapped her legs around his waist tight and began to kiss him. He kicked his door opened and walked toward his bed, laying her gently down while pulling her thong off. Every move, every kiss, every stroke was slow but with force as if he wanted to reach her soul. She could tell he missed her because he took his time like he wanted it to last forever.

As he reached Meagan's spot, she moaned, whispering in his ear that she was about to cum. They climaxed together, and he laid beside her. They talked in the dark on politics, which lead to a minor debate. Meagan hated debating so she got quiet, leaving the room silent for a while. There in the dimly lit room, Charles said, "I will always love you, Meagan Parks."

She replied, "I will always love you, Charles Chapman."

He kissed her lips, pulled the cover over his head, and went downtown; it was time for round two. He stood up and pulled Meagan to the edge of the bed, placing his feet stable on the floor so he could grip her hips and place himself inside of her. He turned her around and began sexing her doggy style, smacking her ass as they both moaned with pleasure.

She woke up the next morning with the sun shining through the window. She saw a picture with him, his daughter, and his child's mother inside a frame that said *Family* next to his television. She quickly got up as she began to feel undesirable feelings from the past. Slight envy and thoughts ran through her head of how that should have been them.

Although Charles wasn't with his child's mother, it was once their desire to have their very own family.

After a couple of months of her and Charles living together, she got pregnant. The advice she received from her family led her to an abortion clinic because they felt she wasn't ready, and at the time, their relationship was a mess. Charles supported her decision, even though he wasn't happy about it. Shortly after, that's when he confessed the other woman was pregnant; however, she had made a choice to keep their baby. The memory recap gave her ill feelings. Her stomach felt like it dropped to her feet from thinking about it. She put on her clothes and then called Paul her driver. She opened the bathroom door as he was showering to let him know she would catch up with him later, knowing in her heart it was closure and goodbye.

When Charles said he would always love her, she believed that to the core. They had gone through so much together. Most of all, they had a history, and Charles always felt after she moved out of her parent's house, he had a duty to make sure she was okay, as well as making sure she was protected after that incident in her senior year.

On New Year's Eve of Meagan's senior year, she was hanging with her best friend, Marisa, and her crew. It was Meagan's first-time meeting Marisa's boyfriend. They all went to see the peach drop that night. After all the excitement died down, Meagan, Marisa, and Marisa's new boyfriend decided to leave. The plan was for Meagan to be dropped off at Charles' house, but she never made it to him. Instead, they were all dropped off at Marisa's boyfriend.

When they got to his apartment, it was two other guys there. Marisa went to the back with her boyfriend and left Meagan with the unfamiliar dudes. One of the guys started talking to her; Meagan was cordial, so she spoke back. After a while, he asked if she wanted to ride to the corner store with him. She was cool with it even though it was cold outside. Meagan had on her favorite blue jeans and blue and white Nike's she had just got for Christmas. She was rocking a coat that stopped at her waist, and the hood had fur on it. Meagan decided to ride with this guy and didn't even know his name or anything about him other than the fact that he said he was eighteen. They got into his old school car, and he turned the heater on proceeding to drive but never pulled out of the complex; he just pulled in a dark area in a secluded parking spot.

He looked at Meagan and said, "Hell, now you not about to act scared after all that teasing you just did, I saw how you were looking at me." Meagan sat with confusion. "Come on now, bust it wide open," he grunted. She wasn't responding as he desired, so he pushed her legs up toward the passenger window. Meagan could barely move because of how she was hemmed up against the door and how her legs were pressed against her chest. She could barely breathe, let alone scream. As he fought to get her pants off, she tried to pull them up as he tried to pull them down while crammed against the door. He finally succeeded in pulling her pants from over her butt. He had on some sweat-pants material bottoms, so it was easy for him to remove his pants. With no hesitation, he pulled his penis out and jammed it inside her. He shoved his genitals into her repeat-edly for about three minutes until he ejaculated. When he finished, he released her legs. She sat up with tears in her eyes, pulled her jeans back up, and faced toward the passenger window.

When they got back to the apartment, she didn't bother to get out. She moved to the back seat as Marisa and her boyfriend walked to the car. He turned the music on and took them to the train station. Nobody said a word. When they got to Marisa's house, she asked Meagan what was wrong?

"Why have you been so quiet?" Marisa asked.

As they laid in the dark on the bed, Meagan replied, "He raped me, Marisa," and she cried uncontrollably.

Marisa started to cry and apologized for what happened; they cried until they fell asleep. The next day when Meagan got home, she washed up and finally was near a phone to call Charles to apologize and explain why she didn't make it. While she was on the phone, he could sense something was wrong. He was having car issues so he couldn't go to her, so he paid his friend to go pick her up and bring her back to him.

When they pulled up to Charles' house, he was standing outside, anxious to see her. When she got out of the car, he hugged her tight and could feel her soft tears on his bare chest. He asked, "Baby, what's wrong?"

Meagan hesitated for a second and looked toward the ground and softly said, "I was raped last night."

He paced back and forth with tears in his eyes. He punched the garage door so hard she thought she broke his hand. He asked so many questions, not giving enough time for her to respond. His mother came outside with concern and saw both of them crying.

"Charles, what's wrong?" she asked, and he cried even harder. She asked them to come inside. When they went into the house, he finally told his mom, and she insisted Meagan call her mom at that moment.

Meagan called, and her mother was upset because she didn't tell her first. Meagan's mom arrived and picked her up, and they didn't say anything in the car. Meagan had already showered, so the rape kit wasn't necessary upon arriving at the hospital, so she was just tested to see if she had been exposed to any diseases. Not too long after she was released to go home.

Her parents took her to the police department to file a report. It was learned through the detective's investigation that the guy was twenty-six years old, and because Meagan was older than sixteen, the process was going to be more strenuous then she thought when it came to pressing charges.

It wasn't a thought to fight or press charges because the detectives had come to the ridiculous conclusion that Meagan was feeling bad because she had a boyfriend and decided that she came up with these allegations. The concern of the family secret of what happened when Meagan was thirteen would have been an issue as well if a more in-depth investigation took place. The family didn't want that situation to come to surface or her to get humiliated in the process, so they closed the case and shielded the family secret. The guy got the chance to go free. Meagan again had to move on as if nothing ever happened.

Chapter Four

NEVER KNEW LOVE LIKE THIS BEFORE

inutes later, Paul was pulling up to Charles's loft. Alexis called reminding her that she had an hour and a half to be at the residential property, where she would be managing an office meeting due to staff replacement. Meagan confirmed she would be there in time and for Alexis to be there with all the necessary paperwork.

After the meeting, everyone had left the office, and Meagan was gathering the last of her items when a handsome guy came in. She immediately apologized, stating the door should have been locked, and the office was currently closed. He continued to go on, saying he had been called to come by to take care of some paperwork. She attempted to help but couldn't find his file.

As she was looking for the file, they had small talk, and he requested for her to remember his name. She smiled and said okay, not thinking much about it. She explained how she would be present at the office until she got everything under control at the property and replaced the staff. The next day, a delivery from Flower Galore came by with the most beautiful flowers and an aroma that made the whole office smell like heaven.

"Meagan Parks?" he asked.

"Those are for me?" she questioned. "How beautiful, but who sent them?" In her head, she thought, *Damn, I must have put it down the other night*. But Charles couldn't have possibly known where she was working. She opened the card, and it read, "Remember my name? Say yes to dinner with me?"

Ibaka, she said to herself and smiled. After turning the office upside down, she finally found his file, which was in a box of dead files. She called him to say thank you for the beautiful flowers, and she took him up on his offer by saying yes to his request for dinner.

The next day, she arrived at his condo in Midtown with a beautiful view of the city. He opened the door with his apron on, and a grin that beamed with happiness. The aroma of the food smelled delicious. He had a couple of guests over, which made her nervous at first because it was his family. She met his brother, Mase, and cousin, Pooh. They cracked jokes about Meagan being special because they had never seen Ibaka go all out as he did.

She laughed as he kicked them out of the house and apologized for them intruding. As he prepared their plates, she glared at the baked chicken, string beans, and potatoes. With a big smile, she was by far impressed, and a man cooking for her was a first. They ate and talked, Ibaka was so intelligent. Meagan never knew until then that she had a list. He was fine, athletically built, smart, no children, could cook, had a job, and his own place. He was talking, and she was mentally checking off on a list that was formulating as he spoke. It was an instant fire within her. He had been celibate for a year. However, the way the night was going, Meagan must have cast a spell because he was about to get some ass that night. He asked what her favorite song was and turned it on. As the instrumentals of *Incomplete* by Sisqo dropped, she stood up, and her hips swayed left to right. He stood up and grabbed one hand and put his other around her waist. They danced in the living room, and at the moment, she felt something within her that she thought she could never feel again. That feeling made her vulnerable to love again. She couldn't explain or express what it was, but she knew she was going to give it her all. The night she did.

Ibaka was a homeowner at CityView, a property Meagan was reconstructing and managing new build contractors on. He was a man with a plan that met every thought in mind of the things she wanted. They spent a lot of time together. She eventually stopped going home and spent many nights at his spot. He was everything a woman could ever ask for. When she would stay over, he would leave notes around the house or make her lunch with a special note. They would meet up during the day just to have a quickie, probably more often than they should have due to her work obligations. But she couldn't get enough of him, and he couldn't get enough of her. It was something about his athletic body and his tight ass. He was so sexy, and his thick luscious lips were so soft and juicy, and he knew exactly how to use them.

If they weren't sexing, he was educating her on things in the world that an average guy who was living on the day by day basis couldn't fathom, but she loved everything he shared, and it was life-changing. He expanded her mindset and made her feel anew on the inside and out. He became her Ebony king, the epitome of what a man was. If he came earlier, it would have been too soon, and any time later, it would have been too late. He was right on time and exactly what Meagan needed.

Chapter Five

BROKEN AND UNHEALED SHIT

wo thousand six was a year full of sex, drugs, lots of drinking, and partying. Destiny, Keisha, Liz, and Meagan were always on the go and into something. At that time, Meagan moved with Destiny and her family for a bit when she left Charles and began moving on with her life.

She got a job at a local retail store that was within walking distance to Destiny's house so she wouldn't have to worry about getting back and forth to work. It seemed like as soon as she left Charles, she got a job the next day. Charles was pissed because that was one of their issues. He couldn't hold everything down with his little paycheck, and she couldn't find anything after leaving her last job.

Charles came to her new job, raising hell as if she planned for things to be that way when it was he who broke their relationship apart in the first place. She felt like this was her second chance of getting her life together, and she wasn't going to let him mess it up for her. The moment Meagan saw Charles standing in front of her at her job, she regretted keeping in touch with him and telling him about it.

Smoking, drinking, and partying were all she wanted to do, and after being exposed to it on a regular basis, it virtually consumed her. Destiny's boyfriend was the plug, so they smoked marijuana for breakfast, lunch, and dinner. Meagan dealt with her loneliness, neglect, and pain with smoking. Her motto was "fuck that shit" when it came to her dealing with anything that sounded like drama. Every time things didn't go right, she said those exact words, then rolled and puffed a joint. It was relaxing, soothing, and even in that dark time in her life, it made her feel like all her troubles were washed away.

On the weekends, she and the girls were at the hottest clubs. They would purchase affordable, yet cute and stylish outfits from a local boutique for their nights out. Even though they were balling on a budget, trust and believe, when they walked in the room, they knew they were the shit. Meagan was the dancer, Destiny rolled the blunts, and Liz was the daring one. Whatever Meagan dared her to do, she did that shit! Keisha was the one who had the skill of making sure dudes brought them drinks and kept them coming throughout the night. If they denied the request, she would roast them and devalue any piece of manhood that existed. They went to Mama's Primetime every Sunday and Royal Peacock on Thursdays. At that time, they were broke balling, living from paycheck to paycheck. Meagan managed to purchase a car, and that's how they got around, but their priorities were jacked up. They would buy an outfit and head to the club with the gas tank on E. They had their weed, Keisha was going to make sure they got their drinks, and the ladies got in free—talking about living the life, so they thought. One night they ran out of gas. They laughed and were far from being embarrassed. Destiny and Keisha talked some guy into helping them, and that didn't even stop them from going out that night. They cranked the car up after he put five dollars in the tank, and they were on their way to their regular spot, Mama's Primetime. They did a lot of crazy things during that time.

They had some fun memories they could always laugh back at and some not so much, but with the irresponsible moments came life lessons. Not having priorities and trying to figure out adulthood without guidance led to driving with no insurance and getting her car towed. Meagan hated asking people for stuff, but if she needed anything, her grandma was the one who got her out of the hole.

Meagan wasn't used to the fast life, so the partying, drinking and smoking, were starting to lead and control her. She was losing herself, and her friends were getting frustrated with her. Destiny's boyfriend Rob looked at Meagan one day and said, "Meagan, this life ain't for you. You're not yourself anymore." For one, she was sober at the time when he made the statement, and for two, he was the plug. So, in her head, his words registered as if she was becoming an addict and she wasn't feeling that at all. It took that moment for her to get herself together, along with getting into an argument with Destiny's father because he had been trying to sleep with her. Meagan had gotten tired of the sexual advances he made and snapped. When she went off, it prompting Destiny's mom to ask for her house key and her to leave.

Meagan moved back with her family and met a police officer at a court date for driving with an expired registration. Girlfriend must have looked so pitiful sitting in court that night that when she walked to her car, the officer approached her and told her he could help with getting rid of the tickets. In the midst of her getting her shit together, he helped her get on track with paying her debt off, getting her car right, and into her career. Officer Lucky got her on with Genesis Investments. He was twenty-four years older than her, very experienced, and established. This was the journey that led her to her destiny. She refused to allow her hurt, pain, betrayal, and loneliness to keep her in bondage. Her energy spiraled like wildfire, and the universe accepted her and allowed her to be herself. She had her career and made the most money she ever made. She got her shit together and never looked backed.

Chapter Six

BABY BLUES

*I*baka and Meagan were moving fast, so fast she quickly got pregnant. His spiritual connection with God had him going crazy. "Pregnant and not married," he yelled. "Unacceptable! We have to go to the courthouse and get married", he insisted.

Meagan was not feeling his plea. She had a vision of what her wedding day would look like, and it sure didn't include the courthouse. He had just met her family, and Meagan wasn't sure how serious they were about each other. It was all still so new. A few days later, they were in the car after picking up his brother Mase from a relative's house when they started arguing. Ibaka was so angry he began to press the gas hard. Meagan slapped him for being so disrespectful in front of his brother to her. The last thing she remembered was when she said, "Ibaka, you weak as fuck!" before the car went into the opposite lane and ran into a truck. Her car was totaled. It was a blessing they all made it out with only a couple of scratches.

The next day while in the hospital, Meagan was told she had a miscarriage, and the baby didn't make it through the crash. She was torn to pieces. Meagan cried for days and nights, not understanding why this was happening to her. Although she was upset, she always believed Ibaka was jumping for joy on the inside because of their current situation and him being concerned about having a baby without being married. A few months later, they were pregnant again. Talking about fertile myrtle and breeding bandit. This time around, he was much calmer and less pressured. They now had a baby on the way and needed to figure out life and their relationship quickly!

Chapter Seven

NEW BEGINNINGS

On their wedding day, they danced to *Share My Life* by Kem. Ibaka sang those words as he rubbed her butt and smiled on the dance floor. They had a beautiful wedding that brought family and friends from all around the U.S. together. They danced, laughed, and ate good. Their wedding day was everything they desired it to be. Meagan had children back to back, causing her to leave her corporate job with Genesis, going from being a senior vice president to a stay-at-home mom—talk about a drastic life-changing experience. Ibaka's businesses were doing well, and they purchased a new residential development that was now fully occupied that needed Meagan's attention. This was a blurred moment in life. She was happy to have healthy children, a beautiful home, a nice car, and a husband. She had everything a woman at thirty-six would want; however, she didn't feel empowered and in charge like she did when she was independent and working as the senior vice president of such a large firm. She had always been independent and did things for herself since she was sixteen. Now she depended solely on her husband, and her security now relied on someone else. It wasn't anything Ibaka had done or said; it was an independent mindset that lived within her, coupled with the fact that she had a hard time trusting. It took her a while to appreciate her new position and to allow her mate to carry them while she took care of the home and their children. They were great business partners. With them moving so fast at the beginning, they didn't get the chance to build a friendship, and they were failing in their marriage because of it. He was never home, and she was overwhelmed with being around children all day and being pulled in different directions trying to be everything to everyone. Their communication was not aligned, and because of the disconnect and her hormones changing, she wasn't interested in pleasing him sexually.

She learned to please herself during her first pregnancy, so she eventually mastered the art of self-pleasure. Meagan began to please herself and explore different areas of her body that released built-up tension. She would imagine Ibaka thrusting her until she exploded. This had become enough for her. She started doing more things for herself, gaining new hobbies, and trying out spontaneous events. Meagan had become comfortable with herself, which led to her forgetting about Ibaka's needs altogether. She was so self-reliant, Meagan forgot to love those she loved most.

Chapter Eight

LOVE VS. LUST

*S*ix years of marital ups and downs, and all the highs and lows, somehow led Meagan into the arms of Ali. Ali was a nice-looking brother, light-skinned, curly hair, with a crooked smile. He was from the West Coast, so his accent had a twang, but she liked it. Their children attended the same faith-based private school, so they called each other spiritual brother and sister. Ali's children often hung out at Meagan's house with her kids.

One day, Ali texted Meagan to ask if he could take the children out one weekend. Meagan agreed, but the conversation continued beyond that. They continued to talk all the time and made an effort to keep each other motivated on their goals and aspirations. She didn't know what it was that drew her to him and him to her, but she liked the attention and entertainment. It was all wrong, but she was curious about him, and she loved the feeling of being wanted again.

Now that it was in the air, Meagan's curiosity urged for more. She met Ali at a motel room one night, on a mission to fulfill her desire. Her head was so in the clouds, nothing else mattered at that moment. She was open, vulnerable, and near risking it all. Ali didn't feel comfortable with moving to the next step with Meagan, so they ended the night after a few kisses. As Ali walked her to her car from the room, she saw Ibaka, her dad, and uncle standing next to her car with the police. As Ali and Meagan walked closer to the car, Ibaka screamed, "Ali!" He couldn't believe it was someone he considered his spiritual brother she had been having an affair with. He was so pissed not only because it was his friend and brother, but the idea of having Meagan at some filthy motel spoke volumes of what he felt she was worth. What Meagan didn't know and found out in the midst of the yelling was that Ali was a married man. Meagan always assumed he was a single father since he never wore a ring or talked about his wife. Ali stood there saying not a word, and Meagan tried to express to Ibaka they should talk somewhere else. People were standing outside of their rooms with cameras, and of course, she was embarrassed, but she also tried to keep matters under control. Ibaka pulled off, and she went home, not knowing how things would unravel.

Ibaka had been tracking her every move after Meagan refused to tell him who she had been talking to. He felt she was lying when he called her, so when he got a ping of where she was, he called her relatives after she didn't answer several of his calls thinking something may have happened to her, never did he imagine she would have been laid up at a spot like that.

The next day, she took the children to school and went back home. Ibaka had come home and asked her to go to their room. He was furious, and his eyes were bloodshot red. His voice was deep, and he was angry. He asked her questions and didn't give her a chance to respond. She proceeded to leave, but he hemmed her up against the door. As things got heated, she pushed him back and opened the door and started to run downstairs to the garage. As she pushed the button to lift the garage door, he pulled her by the hair, yanking her back into the house and closing the door. She pleaded for him just to calm down and relax, but he wasn't trying to hear that. She didn't know why he wanted her in the room, but she fought like hell from being pulled up the stairs. They tussled until they were both tired. He said, "Meagan, I'm about to leave because if I don't, I'm going to kill your ass." She asked if they could just talk. She expressed to him that she and Ali did not have sex. That revelation put him at ease a bit, but he was still angry. Meagan suggested he ask all the questions he had on his heart, and she would answer honestly. He asked and cried as she shared the responses.

Every couple has relationship issues, but Meagan never thought she would have had an affair. She knew what it was like to feel betrayed; she never thought in her heart of hearts she would be on the other side. She felt mixed emotions. A part of her felt bad, but it was also a part of her that felt like karma had come to bite Ibaka in the ass. Although her situation was unintentional, her attitude of not being as sympathetic to how Ibaka was feeling was questionable. You would have thought that it was well planned and carried out, but she was in a vulnerable place, a place in which she had warned Ibaka about. She knew once she stopped caring, things would decline from there because she was the one holding the family together. He had a share in doing dirt for years. Meagan had pleaded for his love and attention after years of feeling neglected and ignored. Someone finally got her attention, and for the first time, she acted on it. Men do shit like this all the time, but they can't deal with it themselves. Meagan had become a reflection of him, and he couldn't handle it.

Chapter Nine

I AM MEAGAN PARKS

If she were to describe herself, she would say Meagan Parks is a phenomenal woman, perfectly imperfect. She was not always the confident woman she had become. As a child, she was shy and stayed to herself. In some ways, she still was that shy girl. Never was she the type to be in a big crowd but known to stand out among one. Due to unjust circumstances, experiences in life, she evolved quickly. She became an energy source of love, passion, and forgiveness. A woman that tried to fix everything and everyone around her but never took steps to heal herself. Love, her greatest strength and weakness. A quality that had been a difficult characteristic to understand and nurture. After having so many people use and abuse her and also being a giving person, she became harden.

She had been surrounded by people she loved all her life that used her good qualities for their benefit. While trying to be a daughter, friend, wife, and mother, somewhere, she realized she didn't know who Meagan was. Yet, she was everything she needed to be for everyone else. Meagan reflected on her life and realized she never put her needs first or took time to heal and love herself. When she realized that fact and how invaluable she was, her confidence rose. The energy that surrounded her was temptation and drama; something that was never an issue for her had now become an issue in life. Women are emotional, and Meagan was a very sensitive and emotional person. She took on burdens that were overwhelming for her. Because of the gravity of the situation, she was irrational, which wasn't the best thing for her to do. Experiences she partook in was a part of who she was, but what she was not. Sexual abuse, betrayal, drugs, sex, infidelity, motherhood, and being a wife could have led her into a route that wasn't the most desirable.

She had suffered from being in dark moments, even considered suicide for not knowing and understanding her purpose in life. After living as a successful single woman, giving it all up for her family was a major transition, not that she had regretted starting a family, but there were some things that she missed, such as her independence. She lost a part of herself along the way, and vulnerability led to bad decisions. Before taking accountability, she had a moment of placing blame and pointing the finger at whoever hurt her for the reason she was in a bad place in life. Because she didn't understand the healing process, she didn't understand it wasn't about pointing fingers. The healing process began with the steps of atonement. When she understood that, she could look at her past and not only move on with forgiveness in her heart for others but forgiveness for herself too. The energy that surfaced became surreal. Your heart can't lie to the universe; therefore, true love and understanding showered her.

Chapter Ten

REVISED LOVE STORY

*I*baka was bruised and wounded from Meagan cheating on him. A lot of men don't believe that insecurity resides within them until it's brought out. He understood his part in the situation, and for that, he made a choice to fight for his wife and family. He knew her value, her importance in his life, and what she meant to him. The love that was within was much greater than their circumstances. Some days were more trying than others, due to things that caused a bad memory, flashback, or reminder. They were trying to re-establish trust, but it was a hard journey. Two years after the incident, Meagan and Ibaka decided to have a small ceremony to renew their vows and their commitment to each other. On that day, they chose each other after choosing the higher being first in their lives.

There is someone destined for every person to walk the journey of life with, and they were each other's missing part of the puzzle. It took them to hurt each other to understand that deep down, true love is what they were running away from all along.

This time around, they aimed to love each other the

right way by first blocking out all the outsiders. Second, making each other a priority. Third, communicating effectively with love and respect. And fourth, being intentional with their love languages. With change came growth and their growth led to a powerhouse that created a legacy of greatness.

Chapter Eleven

IS THIS YOU HURT? ARE YOU THERE HAPPINESS?

*H*appiness, what does that feel like?
It seems so easy but yet unreachable.
Happiness, are you there?
All I feel is hurt and pain.
Sex, drugs, drinking is this you hurt?
You see, there is a story behind those pretty smiles.
But as a strong person, you can't walk around with a frown.

As human beings, we have to understand it's okay not to be OKAY. It's necessary for us to take a moment to understand our mind frame before moving on in life. Before you know it, you'll be piling pain on top of pain. Drinking and smoking will be a source of escape. Sex will be used for self-pleasure rather than the science of bringing two souls together to bring about a strong connection.

Is this you hurt?
Where have I gone wrong?
I admit I made a mistake.
I confess my fault, God.
The regret and remorse are felt strongly.

As an imperfect person, apologize to those that have been hurt in the journey of your pain.

Forgive those who have caused you pain.

Restoration and reconciliation are what has brought about peace

and for that, the higher being is pleased.

Are you there happiness?

It's not about placing the blame. It's about atonement. We say we understand who we are as individuals and believe we have healed from our own personal trauma. But hurt people, hurt people. Even when you feel you are on the rise, your relationship with others will have a pattern that will identify what's really within. Open your eyes and make the necessary steps to heal your brokenness. You owe it to yourself and those you truly love to be released from the hurt and for it to be transferred into true happiness, which is the secret of beauty inside and outside.

Is that you happiness? Because hurt doesn't live here anymore.

ABOUT THE AUTHOR

Author Ashley Poole considers herself a true reflection of a butterfly. She went from barely passing in high school with a 2.0 to graduating from American InterContinental University Summa Cum Laude and now a successful Real Estate Agent. Proud wife of Nigeria Poole and mother to Mekhi, Maliq, and Mecca and god-mother to Ariana, this Boynton Beach, Florida native now resides in Atlanta, Georgia. Her greatest attributes are helping people and giving back to her community. In her spare time, you can find her traveling, working out, and exploring new places to eat.

If I were to give my younger self advice on anything, I would say, "love yourself deep, because you are love." We seek things from others that we are capable of and responsible for giving ourselves. When we understand that, we can lead with strength and faith that eliminates fear.